Fifth Blade

V. B. BAILEY

authorHOUSE®

AuthorHouse™
1663 Liberty Drive
Bloomington, IN 47403
www.authorhouse.com
Phone: 1-800-839-8640

Published by AuthorHouse 7/30/2013

ISBN: 978-1-4817-7420-8 (sc)

*To my Heavenly Father, who
gave me something more precious
than anything on this earth*

PREFACE

Living to glorify my Father is my goal.

I don't have all of the answers, but I do have a lot of faith and love for my Heavenly Father. I want to share this love with the world because this is what I do know. I have a pearl. You can have it too.

CHAPTER I

The End of Time

I woke up early in the morning from a dream that was too real. It was unbelievable because it felt as though it wasn't a dream. I had to rush to find a notebook to put the events of the dream on paper so that I wouldn't forget what happened in the dream.

Here's what I wrote:

> I remembered walking with my husband;
> or it seems as though it was my husband.
> All of a sudden, we heard lots of noise.
> People around us were looking up into
> the sky. We both looked up and saw birds
> covering the sky. The multitude of birds
> was so great their clustered bodies seemed

to block out the sun. Other strange things were happening all around us. I can't remember all of the details of what I saw in the dream, but I remember saying, "This must be the end of time."

Everyone panicked and ran for safety. Everyone was terrified because the birds were flying low to the ground and were just everywhere.

This dream took place in October 2008. For some reason, I didn't write down a specific date, which is unusual, as I normally record everything that I write in my journal, even down to the time that I'm writing.

I grabbed my husband and picked him up and flew to what or where I thought was safe. It appeared as though I was on a roof where there was a covering from the birds' attack.

Now, when I said I flew, I do mean that I flew. But that's not a strange thing. I dream about flying all the time and rescuing people or just flying to assist someone in danger. I know this sounds strange, but it was my dream. I don't want to get sidetracked about that because that's not the true issue here.

Just take a few minutes and finish reading about the dream. Weird, I know. But it's a dream.

> While sitting on this roof, I started to pray to God. In my heart, I knew that my faith in God would keep us safe, but I had to get myself focused and release the fear so that I would think clearly. I wanted everyone to escape these scary birds. Then I realized a woman was trying to climb up to where we were on the roof. I don't know why I didn't just go and get her. But I had somehow gotten other people on the roof with me.
>
> We were encouraging this woman not to give up but to keep climbing. It seemed as though she kept looking back. I reached for her hand, and she couldn't seem to reach me. We saw her fall straight to the ground. But she didn't seem to be hurt. I kept talking to her, but other than my telling her to fight the birds off of herself, I don't remember the whole conversation. She looked up at us as though she was okay. Then all of a sudden, I watched what appeared to be a spirit come from her body.
>
> It seemed as though, just before we witnessed this happening (her falling), I

had decided to go down or fly down to get her.

So, as I flew down from the roof, I met up with this spirit. I felt the spirit go right past me. I could hear someone yell to me that the spirit just passed by me. And I replied, "Yes, I know."

I was back on the roof, and I was looking at all the people on the ground still fighting the birds. There seemed to be so many people looking up at us on the roof wanting to be rescued. I heard many of the people yelling and crying.

For some reason, one particular woman caught my attention because she knew my name and kept yelling something to me. It was as though she wanted my attention more than anyone else did. She appeared to be a well-groomed woman. I don't remember anyone else's clothes, so why she stood out, I don't know. But I remember praying with all of my might for the birds to fly away and to leave the crowd of people alone. I just wanted everyone to be safe, and I didn't know how to save everyone, but I wanted to try anyway. I prayed for direction.

The woman kept on trying to get my attention. After flying down to where she was standing in the midst of the flying birds, I reached out to her to pick her up (from the crowd) to bring her up to our safe haven. I grabbed her hands tightly to get a good grip on her, and immediately, I felt a strange sensation go through my body.

Her clothing fell off of her, and a spirit of darkness came out and told me to stop telling people about God. The evilness had a grip on me that was very strong. It told me to be afraid, and I said, "No, I will not be afraid." It said, "I can't destroy you if you aren't afraid of me." I fought back and told the spirit to let me go. I told it that it had no power over me and that I was covered by the blood. The dark spirit's strong grip on me was intense, and I could barely move. But then, for some reason, I felt a soothing presence of an angel or something surround me as I continued to fight my way away from this dark spirit and to get back to the rooftop for safety.

Something caught my eye. The people on the ground witnessed the same thing. No one was saying anything. Out of the corner

of my eyes, I saw a tall, young boy come
from the sky to my left. He appeared to be
about twelve to fifteen years old. It was as
though he was a giant child. Then, to his
right, I saw a man dressed in white. I saw
no color in either of the faces. The man
too was a giant. They were both dressed
in white linen. But the two of them stood
there and watched me fight with the dark
spirit. For some reason, the birds weren't
of any concern anymore. But the dark
spirit was the battle. I could sense that
its purpose was to scare all of us. I was
startled, but something inside of me would
not let me give up. It was as if I wasn't
fighting by myself. While in the battle, I
heard the spirit say, "Be afraid because I
am here to kill."

The spirit said many ugly words and
wanted me to be afraid of him. I refused.
He was so angry with me.

I used the pronoun *he* in the journal as I wrote
this, so that's why I'll be referring to this spirit as
a male.

The spirit tried to smother my mouth
so that the word of God wouldn't come
out, but I still got them out. And though

my words appeared to be unclear, he understood everything I said. The spirit's grip was very powerful, but my will was even more powerful. I was determined not to be afraid and to fight back. The dark evil spirit just kept saying, "Why aren't you afraid of me?" We were locked in close combat. The scripture about resisting the devil and he shall flee was in my heart. I repeated it continuously. I told him, "I will not fear you; you are a liar." The fight became about my faith in God. I had to exercise and use my weapons of warfare now. What was most important about this encounter was our exchange of words. I knew that I couldn't give up because this battle was about my faith.

Then all of a sudden, he was gone. I looked to my left and saw the giant child and the giant man still standing there. I was thinking, *Why did they just stand there and watch me fight?* Then they disappeared.

Then the people with me begin telling me that the dark spirit had put nails through my mouth. I remember touching my mouth and saying, "But I don't feel it." Then I saw the nails fall slowly from my mouth. I never felt any pain in my mouth. I felt tired yet so happy that this fight was over.

When I woke up, I actually felt tired, as though the events in my dream had really happened.

What a dream.

CHAPTER 2

A Home

On September 17, 2007, I closed on a beautiful house. My husband and I had watched the house as it was being built. It was more of a dream house to him than it was to me. We both enjoyed watching it being built from the ground. When we actually got into the house about late October or the first of November, we still couldn't believe that it was our home. We decided not to share the news with any of our family members until we got the house decorated. We had planned a big Christmas party to celebrate our new home, as well as our birthdays; mine is right before Christmas, and his is right after Christmas.

So we decided that we would surprise everyone. We told everyone that they were invited to a big

Christmas party at one of our close friend's house. The plan went very well, and everyone (except my mother) was very surprised. My mother knew it was our house because she knew that I had been looking for a house for a very long time. She wasn't too surprise that the house was ours, but she was surprised about the size of our new home.

This was the first time in our marriage that we seemed to be happy and not arguing about something all the time. We both were willing to work extra hard to pay for the huge mortgage, as well as to decorate our beautiful home.

About a week after the party, I was in the kitchen cooking dinner. The back door opened, and I turned to watch my husband on his knees, actually crawling into the kitchen. I stopped in my tracks and ran over to see what was wrong with him. He said that he was very tired and feeling terribly. I told him that he had to make an appointment to go to the doctor the next day. It was late at night, and he had worked all day. He went up stairs to take a shower while I continued to prepare his dinner.

He ate and went to bed. He had a bad cold and was coughing a lot. We thought he had the flu.

He and I went to see his primary physician the next day, and the doctor decided to run some tests. The receptionist scheduled the first set of tests, but in the meantime, my husband felt well enough to go back to work. The results from the first tests were inconclusive, so on his birthday, his doctor decided to do another test, which would require him to be hospitalized.

I was in the cafeteria trying to get something to eat when the doctor called me on my cell phone to give me the results. I immediately lost my appetite when I realized it was the doctor. I could barely hold the cell phone in my hand. He told me over the phone that my husband was out of surgery and that he would have the results in a few days. He also told me that he suspected one of two things.

On January 4, 2008, we went to see his doctor. The staff person at the front desk put us in a small waiting room. The doctor and the nurse came into the room, and the nurse stood extremely close to me. I thought to myself how friendly they both were. His doctor sat in his chair very close to my husband. I remembered thinking, *He is awfully close to him, but maybe that's how he talks to his patients.*

He told us to go with him to view the X-ray results. He showed us something, but neither of us really understood. Then he took both of us back to his office, where he and his nurse positioned themselves very close to the both of us. I began to think that something was wrong then.

The doctor started to explain to us what was on the X-ray, and then he said that it was fourth-stage cancer—terminal. We both screamed out at the same time and cried. Our worlds seemed to be collapsing. And at the same time, what had been separate worlds had united and become one—together.

The nurse took me out of the room, and the doctor stayed with my husband. I can't explain what my husband must have felt, but I felt as though I could feel his agony. It was the worst day ever. I thought about all of our marital problems, and they didn't matter anymore. Before the nurse took me out of the room, I looked at my husband and saw his fear. I hurt for him so much, almost as if it were me. No words could explain what happened in that room on January 4, 2008. I will never ever forget that day. How could what he'd thought was a bad cold be terminal cancer? I became a different person on that day. Love took over me—you know, that agape love, true love for my husband. All I could think about was how he felt. No words could comfort him.

From that day, every aspect of our lives changed. I have to stop to compose myself even as I remember that horrible day. It's still hard to deal with now.

But that's not all that we had to deal with during the fight for his life. Where was there room for anything else to deal with at this stage? It can't get any worse than this you have to think.

Well, it does.

CHAPTER 3

Chemo

We prepared ourselves for the first day of chemo; we had been informed that we would be at the center all day. When we got there, both of us just stood still in amazement at seeing how many people were there for treatment. On that particular day, my husband was the youngest person at the clinic. We noticed that most of the people were elderly, at least where we were seated. Then we were told to come to the back room, and then we saw young kids. Seeing so many young kids with cancer was devastating. It was a very sad atmosphere. My first thought was, *All of these people are fighting to live.*

As my husband's infusion of chemo began, I just watched him. I couldn't determine if he wanted to cry or just float with the moment. All I knew was that I had to be strong for him and keep him motivated to push through for his life. The atmosphere in the center was grim, at least to me. I just couldn't help thinking that I wished I had the ability to touch everyone and everyone would be healed. I had to excuse myself and go into the restroom to cry. I couldn't take anymore at that moment. In the restroom, I just cried and cried. I had to get it out because I couldn't let my husband see me break down. He was depending on me, so there was no time for my emotions to get the best of me. I knew that we had a long road to travel. The doctor had already explained to me that it wasn't going to be easy because the chemo was going to make him weak, at least for the first three days after each session.

When I got back to the Infusion room, he had fallen asleep. I was so glad to see him resting. I just let him sleep because I knew we had at least five more hours to go. As I sat there watching him, I couldn't help wondering how in the world we were going to make it financially with all the bills we had and especially with the new house. I had recently gotten my license to operate my own staffing company, but that wasn't going to happen. I needed a real job where I could count on the money coming in on a regular basis. Yet, I needed to be with my husband every day while he was going through the chemo treatments. I tried to turn off my thoughts about my responsibilities and my need to get a job because I couldn't leave him. I decided that this wasn't an option. I made up my mind on that first day of his chemo that I would not leave his side throughout this fight.

The nurses at the center were wonderful. They did everything to make sure that everyone was comfortable and had whatever he or she needed for the long stay. It seemed that each patient had a lot of support from family and friends. People were coming and going so they could sit with their loved ones. At that point in each patient's life, I'm sure that having people there to support them made a difference.

As for us, my husband didn't want anyone there except for me. I know that his family would have been there if he had asked, but he told me that he just wanted me there. At that time, he wanted only me by his side so that, if he broke down, no one else would see that side of him.

Now believe me, the intimacy in his desire to rely on me was new. We'd had lots of issues in our marriage. But now, we had to put all of that aside and focus on him getting better.

CHAPTER 4

A Monster

It had taken about three months of chemo treatments before the doctor reported to us any change in his diagnosis. The doctor said that the lymph nodes had shrunken some, and that was good news. My husband had actually started to gain weight and didn't look as though he was in fourth-stage cancer. He looked very healthy. The treatments made him weak, but he still looked quite handsome.

The doctor decided that he wanted to try a new trial drug on my husband. We were warned of the side effects. His face started to break out, and he was prepared for that to happen. However, some weeks after he'd taken the trial drug, his face began to look as though he had turned into a monster. He was extremely upset that the doctor had not told him the degree to which the drug would disfigure him. Everywhere we went people would stop and stare at him. No one wanted to get close to him because he looked as though he had some type of horrible disease. This made him even more depressed, and our lives seemed to be spiraling downward. I did everything I could to reassure him that the condition of his face didn't matter to me. I knew it was the drugs in his system. I would even rub his face to let him know that I wasn't afraid to touch him. Every time we went to the doctor, he would say that the drug was supposed to have that side effect—that it meant the drug was in his system. But that was not comforting to my husband. He didn't want to look like a monster out of a horror story. That's how he felt, and he didn't even want to go out of the house. I couldn't blame him. Looking in the mirror hurt him terribly.

After my husband had taken this trial drug for about two months, the doctor decided to take him off of it because of the side effects. We had to make a special trip to the doctor's office to sign papers stating that we had been updated on the recent findings about the drug. The only result of this drug was the devastating role its side effect had played on my husband's mental state.

I became very concerned about my husband's mental state because I began to see things that needed to be addressed, but I was afraid to question him about these concerns. I knew that it was important not to confront him about anything else. He had enough to deal with at that point, and addressing his now strange behavior didn't seem appropriate at the time.

Even though I tried not to leave him too much in the house by himself, I needed to get away; so I went for a walk one day just to get myself together. I really needed help with his peculiar behavior, but I couldn't tell anyone. I just had to deal with it and keep my mouth closed. I just kept thinking, *This is my husband and it is my responsibility to take care of him no matter what he does or says right now. He needs me and I will deal with his mood swings and anything else that happens.*

When I returned home, after walking for about an hour, I noticed a change in my husband's behavior. While I was out walking, I had called to check on him, and he'd told me that it was good for me to get out of the house for a little while and had said that he was going to use his computer to get online. He had been in a good mood then, and now that I'd returned, his mood had changed. He was still on the computer, but now he was surly and frustrated. I don't know what happened while I was gone.

I started praying immediately, asking God to give me the strength to deal with his behavior. I just kept smiling and tried to comfort him. I talked to him about what he was trying to find online. I knew that he was looking for information about taking some online classes, as well as contractors to do some work in the house. He said that he didn't want me to help him because this would give him something to focus on right now. When I started to ask him questions about his search, he would get smart and say ugly things. I just walked away because I knew that he was not having a good day, again.

This did upset me, but it was nothing new. I had been dealing with his mood swings for a while now. It just seemed to be worst now, and I understood that he had a reason to be angry. So, there was nothing that I could say. It wasn't about me. My life revolved around him now.

CHAPTER 5

An Outlet

After some months of chemo, my husband was able to function enough to try to work a little bit, at least for a couple of hours. He had gotten one of his friends to work with him for a few hours running cable wires into his customers' homes. This required lifting a heavy ladder, which he could no longer do by himself. He was a very strong man, and he loved to work before he got sick, so his weakened state was extremely hard to deal with. He was independent, and he hated depending on anyone to help him every time he had a job to do. This made him extremely depressed and moody.

"Workaholic" would be a true description of him. I think the hardest thing for him to accept at that point in his life was becoming weaker and weaker and not being able to perform his daily routine of working from sun up to sun down. He often expressed to me that he felt so weak and he had a hard time accepting this change in his life.

It was almost the end of 2008, yet it seemed as though it was yesterday when the doctor had told him that he had terminal cancer. The year seemed to be a nightmare that both of us were in and couldn't wake up from. We spent so much time together that year. In fact, this was the first time in our marriage that we had spent every single day together. I couldn't go to work because I had to be there for him. I also didn't want to leave him because I was afraid about his emotional state, as well as his physical being. He needed help with both. The doctor had told us that my husband's mental state would change, and I realized that his prediction was now coming true. I knew that I had to get additional help so that we could find ways to cope with my husband's ailing mental state. Doing so was about my survival as well now; I had experienced things that were becoming a little scary.

I decided to start working on my book. Writing had been a passion of mine for a very long time. This was a good outlet for me. It allowed me to escape the sadness around me.

While sitting in bed, trying to put my thoughts in words, I couldn't help but think about my own state of being. Despite having been on a diet and counting calories for the previous two months, I had gained a lot of weight. My stomach was big, and I was not used to that. I had always had relatively big thighs, but my stomach and waistline had been small most of my life. But then I started to think about my husband and realized that I had bigger fish to fry. It just wasn't about me anymore. The fact that I was not pleased with my appearance, especially the circles under my eyes from loss of sleep every night, could not be a concern right now. I was responsible for my husband, and that was all that mattered.

And let's not talk about the fact that I was possibly going through menopause. I knew that I had no time to be concerned about myself. I just floated through each day. I put all of my energy into my husband. He was my priority, and I just wanted him to get better. Even though I felt utterly exhausted, I had to keep pushing through. All I could do was pray and pray and pray, every day.

Some days seemed harder than others. These were not the days that he felt bad. These were the days that he felt better. Odd, I know. If my husband felt better and was not in a lot of pain, these were the days that I caught hell from him. He would be so mean—yes, mean. I would ask him sometimes if he had turned into someone else, because that's what it seemed like to me. When he was really sick, he was nicer. But heaven help me, if he felt better, he was a different man. Go figure.

I just dealt with the good and the bad. Crying out to God seemed to be the only answer. I did a lot of praying. What else was there to do? I still loved my husband, no matter what, for good or bad.

CHAPTER 6

The Ceiling Fan

On December 28, 2008, I decided to lie down on the sofa in the family room. It was late at night, and all of the lights were off. My husband was upstairs sleeping. I just stared at the ceiling in deep thought. I then closed my eyes for a while and thought about the year we'd had and the things we were dealing with presently. I felt overwhelmed. I had to be responsible for my husband, the mortgage on the new home, the empty rental property in the city, and the back taxes that were piling up. The fact that my son was still in college and I had to figure out how to keep him in college was a significant concern as well.

After opening my eyes to see the dark room, my focus went straight to the ceiling fan. I wasn't thinking about any problems. I just stared at the ceiling fan for some reason. My focus turned to the fan's blades. I remembered purchasing the fan and having it installed. I'd had to special order it because I'd wanted a special color and style. But that wasn't the reason I was staring at the ceiling fan. I was looking directly at the blades, and I noticed that it only had four blades. This detail caught my attention so much that I got up from the sofa and stood up in the dark room. I saw four blades. But I knew that couldn't be right. The ceiling fan that I had purchased and had installed had five blades. I knew that, and I kept telling myself that it did. But looking directly at the blades, I could see only four. I kept saying to myself, *How in the world can this be possible?* "There is a fifth blade, and I know that with all of my heart," I said out loud. I had purchased the fan and had seen it being installed, so why in the world couldn't I see the fifth blade? Where had it gone? No one could tell me that it didn't exist. I was getting a little beside myself now because I knew that I was right; yet what I was seeing was not the truth. I couldn't accept what I saw.

I stood there trying to figure this out, and then I closed my eyes and looked again. It was dark, but I saw four blades—not five. I noticed that the light from the night-light allowed me to have the visual of the four blades. "Okay then," I said. "I was wrong.

There is no fifth blade. I just thought it was there when I purchased it from the store. I am just tired and not thinking right," I told myself.

I lay back down and accepted that fact. I was okay with being wrong. But then something inside me kept saying, *There is another blade.* I got up again and looked around the room to see what the little night-light was allowing me to see. I couldn't see much in the room, but I saw the four blades on the ceiling fan. I looked at the night-light again, and then I saw what looked like a reflection from the night-light. I refocused my eyes and looked again at the blades.

"Oh my gosh! There's the fifth blade," I said. The reflection from the night-light had covered it. I had known it was there. I immediately thought about my faith in God and I knew what this experience meant.

You see, I couldn't see the blade, but I knew it was there. In my heart, no matter what we were going through, I knew that I had to continue to stand and believe that God was with us during this trial. This was my hope, and I wasn't going to let go, no matter what the outcome. That fifth blade was going to be symbolic of the days and years to come. No matter what happened, no matter what I saw, I had to hold onto my faith because sometimes you can see and still not see the truth.

CHAPTER 7

The Polygraph Test

We managed to keep the mortgage payment going for all of 2008, even though I wasn't working. My husband was still trying to work part-time, but the mortgage was getting harder and harder to pull together. I had used up every credit card we had to pay bills, and I couldn't borrow any more money from my family. I had applied for so many jobs, and I was waiting to take a polygraph test for the government job that I had gotten. I was very glad that I was being considered, even though the job was in Washington, DC, and I would be commuting every day; I didn't mind. My husband was getting a little stronger now, and he could work more hours, just not by himself. His partner would go out on the truck with him, and my husband would do the lightweight jobs.

In the beginning of January 2009, I had to go back to retake the polygraph test. I had been extremely nervous the first time. I couldn't get my husband off of my mind, yet I wanted this job badly. I had worked for this agency over twenty years ago, and I had dreamed of going back once my son graduated from high school.

On the day that I went back to take the polygraph again, I was so nervous that I could barely hold myself together. I couldn't understand why the first one wasn't good enough. I knew that I didn't do drugs or even drink alcohol. I had lived a simple life and tried to be a good citizen, so why was there a problem with the polygraph anyway?

Well, the second polygraph was horrible. I asked the man who was doing the polygraph not to put the strap on me so tightly because the last time it was so tight that it actually made my ribs sore. I realized after I asked him that he would probably be offended, and I wished that I hadn't made that comment. He asked me my age several times, and I thought that was odd. But I assumed that this was a way to test whether I was telling the truth. I kept thinking that I hoped my age wasn't a determining factor in me getting the job.

The results of the test still weren't favorable. I don't know why. I told him everything about myself and didn't hold back anything. I explained to him what was going on with my husband and that I really needed this job because of our finances. He asked me about filing bankruptcy, and I remember saying something about my concerns about that if I did not get this job. Even though my husband and I had never discussed filing bankruptcy at that point, I knew that keeping the mortgage payment current would be a problem if I wasn't gainfully employed. I shouldn't have said that either because you couldn't have bankruptcy on your credit report if you were to work with this government agency. I was hanging myself all the time and didn't even realize that I was doing so at the time. I just wanted to tell the truth, and I wanted this job. I guess I thought that, in a perfect world, the agency's representatives in charge of hiring would see that I needed this job and, after examining my background, that I would be eligible for employment with the agency. In fact, as the polygraph examiner was asking me questions, I couldn't help thinking about how I had tried to be a good American citizen, so why should I be so nervous about this polygraph, outside of my husband's fight for his life? My credit was still good at that point.

But now, after so many years have passed since that day in January 2009 when I received my letter from the agency rescinding my offer of employment, I realize why I wasn't a good candidate for employment with them. I had baggage. I wouldn't have been focused, and I would have had too much going on in my life to be totally dedicated to my job. At least I believe that is, in part, why I didn't get the job. Of course, I was very upset about not getting the job I so desperately wanted at the time. I even tried to appeal, to no avail. The agency's decision wasn't acceptable to me because I was a hard worker, I was stable, and I had a sound mind. I cried for many days, but I had to stay strong for my husband, who depended on me every day.

Hindsight is funny because the same week that I received the letter acknowledging that I was no longer being considered for that job, I got a call from a temporary agency offering me a long-term assignment. I started that job in January 2009. And now, years later (2012), I have only taken off one week from work. I didn't really want the assignment, but I needed a job, and the pay was good. I believe going to work every day was an outlet for me because I had to stay focused while at work in order to be successful.

Every morning I would leave the house to go to this job, which was about twenty-five miles away. My husband would get up and prepare my lunch and see me off to work. I didn't want to leave him all day, but I had no choice at that point. By the time I got home every day, he would have dinner prepared. He tried to keep busy and would go out every day just to get out of the house.

CHAPTER **8**

Disney World

After about five months of working, I began to notice that my husband was getting weaker and weaker. I remember coming home late one day to find him waiting for me on the steps. He broke down and cried, saying that he was scared and wanted me to hold him. We cried together for about fifteen minutes, and then we talked about having his mother come to stay with him. The doctor had arranged for me to contact a nurse if my husband's condition worsened. Needing someone to sit with him to ensure that he was getting the proper amount of oxygen, I made the call.

My husband was not happy about the nurse coming around. The doctor advised me that I needed to put a bed downstairs because he would be getting too weak to go up and down the stairs. We both got scared. After the bed was placed in the room, my husband decided to close the door and to stay out of that room. He told me that he knew that he would one day die in that bed and that he was not going in that room at all. I put blinds on the French doors that led to that room so that he could not see the bed, and he continued to go up the stairs to the bedroom. It was hard for him, but he climbed the stairs anyways, just very slowly. He was determined not to use that bed.

One day while I was in the kitchen cooking, I heard him calling out to me to help him. He could not get up the steps. He could not breathe. I ran for the oxygen, and we just sat there on the steps. He was hysterical and cried out like a child. His agony broke my heart. I tried so hard not to cry, but I couldn't hold the tears back. I wanted to hold him close to me, but he could barely breathe. I told him that I would call hospice. A hospice worker who had visited our home had given me a telephone number to call if I needed help. He refused, telling me to just let him get the oxygen we had in the room and he would be okay. I did.

Once he made it to the bed upstairs, I saw that he needed medicine to calm him down. I gave him what the doctor had prescribed, and he drifted off to sleep. I decided to call hospice anyway to make sure that I was doing the right thing.

After I explained to the nurse what had happened, she advised me to keep him from going up and down the steps. I told her that I had tried to stop him, but he was adamant about not going in that room with the downstairs bed. I just couldn't stop him.

Even though my husband was now on oxygen every day at that point, he decided that he wanted to go to Disney World. He made all of the necessary arrangements for the flight, and we made preparations to go in August 2009. I talked with the hospice nurse, and she made arrangements with another hospice facility in Florida for me if I needed any assistance.

She said that the agency would give us enough oxygen to take with us, and if we needed more while in Florida, I could contact the hospice representative in Florida. I knew that traveling in his condition would be hard on him, but he wanted to go anyway.

We did. It was a struggle. We had a connecting flight and had to walk a long way to board the flight to Florida. All I could think about was how in the world he would make it through the terminal. He needed a wheelchair, but he would not let me get one. As we made our way through the airport to get to the connecting flight, it got to the point that he could barely breathe. I wanted to turn around and go back home because it was just too much. But he was determined that we were going to Disney World.

He told me to walk ahead of him to make sure that we didn't miss the flight. I did. We were lucky; I found out that the connecting flight was delayed. I was so glad to go back to get him and to tell him that he could stop and rest a while because the flight was about an hour late. What a break.

It was about two o'clock in the morning by the time we got to our room in Florida. I asked him to let me call hospice because he didn't look too well. He was struggling to breathe, even with the oxygen, but he said no. He just wanted to go to bed, and he insisted that he would be okay if he got some rest.

The next day, we had to stay in the room most of the day because it was too hot for him to go out and he was still very tired. Later on that evening, he decided that he wanted to try to go out and get dinner. We had a stove in our room, but we needed to go to the grocery store. We made it to the grocery store and picked up a few things for dinner. He couldn't eat much because he couldn't keep much in his stomach. I had lost my appetite because I saw that he was suffering. Watching him struggle to breathe and not being able to do anything to make it better was so difficult.

Once we decided to go to the theme park, we geared up with enough oxygen to last him for a couple of hours. It was so hot though. It must have been about 95 degrees that day. If not, it surely felt that way. As my husband and I walked through the theme park, we had to stop about every fifteen minutes so he could cool off inside a restaurant or store. I knew that he was overdoing it, but he was determined to press through.

We finally made it to the parade. I watched him the entire time. He was like a child. He kept saying that he couldn't believe that he had made it to Disney World; for a long time, he had wanted to go and had never had the chance. Watching him at one point was like watching my child experience a dream come true. He was so happy, yet I knew that he was wishing that things were different. He even said to me that he felt like a little boy whose dream had come true. At that point, I was glad that we made the trip to Disney World.

After we left the parade, he was ready to go back to the room. He was exhausted. Once we got back to the room, he just rested. He decided that we needed to talk about some things. The conversation was very serious. He wanted us to make plans for our life. He said that he wasn't going to die and that we were going to spend time traveling and enjoying each other. He said that he was going to take some classes so that he could try to get an office job. He knew that he couldn't do any more laborious work at that point. He told me that he wasn't going to leave me.

All we could do was just hold each other, and we were so thankful for that quiet time together. It meant so much to both of us. We were filled with hope for our future together.

The trip home was absolutely hard on him. I was so frightened on the plane because he could barely breathe at one point. I wanted to let the flight attendant know that he needed help, but he said that he would try to push through. He did.

Once we got back home, he got worse. I really believe that the trip was too much for him.

CHAPTER 9

TheModification

In the process of going through a modification for our mortgage, I had to keep sending paperwork to the mortgage servicing company. It was so frustrating. We didn't know what to expect. The bank kept asking for more and more paperwork. There were days that I couldn't go to the mailbox for fear of losing our home. The phone calls came in daily. Certified mail kept coming, and the threat of foreclosure hovered over us daily. I knew that my husband couldn't deal with this, so I had to handle it on my own. It was important that he didn't have any extra problems, yet I knew he too was very concerned about losing our home. I told him to let me handle the mortgage and said that he needed to stay focused on getting well.

By October 2009, my husband was waking up sick every night around two o'clock in the morning. I had to get up at 5:00 a.m. to get ready to go to work. So, most nights I only got about four hours of sleep, if that. I was exhausted every day, but I had to push through. I couldn't afford to miss a day of work. If I didn't work, I didn't get paid. We needed every dime at that point.

The fight for the modification was a real battle. Every time I turned around, the bank wanted more paperwork. Now, they wanted information that required my husband to reach out to his accountant. At this point, his mother was staying with us. I had to work long hours, and he needed someone there with him.

One particular day in November, I had to work on Saturday for about four hours. My husband said that he felt strong enough to go to his accountant's office to get the paperwork. I got back home around 11:30 a.m. He was not doing well. I could see that he was very weak. I told him that I would go to the accountant's office to get what we needed for the modification. The mortgage company had given us a timeframe—we were to have the paperwork completed by November 20, which was just around the corner.

Despite the fact that we needed the paperwork for the bank, I was more concerned about my husband's condition. He didn't have much energy, but he was very determined to go to the accountant's office by himself. He said that he could handle it by himself. His mother begged him and I begged him not to go because he was struggling to breathe.

He decided that I could drive him, and I told him that his mother needed to go with us as well. I knew that, if he got sick while I was driving, I might not be able to do what needed to be done. So he decided that his mother could ride with us to the accountant's office.

It took an incredibly long time to get the paperwork done at the accountant's office—so long that I had to tell the accountant we had to leave because my husband was running out of oxygen. He had taken only one small portable tank to the accountant's office because he wasn't planning on being there too long.

By the time the accountant was wrapping up, my husband looked as though he was almost going in and out of consciousness. His head kept falling back as though he was sleep. I said at that point that we were leaving. The accountant saw what was happening and quickly finished the paperwork.

CHAPTER 10

Fighting for Life

By the time we got home, things took a drastic turn. I was so glad that his mother was with us. He needed oxygen now. As soon as I pulled into the garage, I told his mother that I was going into the house to see if he had any more small tanks of oxygen left. He didn't. Then I remembered that hospice had made the cord to the large oxygen tank long enough to reach upstairs because he had refused to sleep in the bed downstairs. I ran for the oxygen mask and the cord to take to the garage.

Even after we'd given him oxygen, he still could not get out of the car. We didn't know what to do. His mother kept calling him by his name. He said he couldn't get up. He could barely talk.

My adrenaline had kicked in at that point, and I was determined to do whatever it took to revive my husband. I had to get him out of the car. I grabbed his upper body and physically lifted him from his seat. His mother could only watch. He was conscious but extremely weak. He told me that he didn't want me to hurt my back lifting him, and I told him not to worry about me. I told him that I was going to get him to the bed so that he could get some rest from the long trip.

I had to put him in the bed downstairs because he most definitely couldn't climb the steps to the bedroom, and I couldn't lift him up the stairs. He didn't resist getting into the bed downstairs. I believe that, at that point, he was just glad to be home and wanted to get into bed to get some rest. After a while, he started to talk better.

He told me that he wanted cable in that room so that he could watch some Westerns on the television. He called the cable provider himself and asked them to install the cable. He told me to go into the garage and get some cable wires to put in the living room so that the cable would be long enough to reach the room that hospice had sat up for him. He actually got out of the bed to tend to this and make sure that the cable wire would reach from the living room to the room where the bed was placed. Now, that doesn't sound like a person who is fighting for his life. He was that determined that he was going to live and beat the cancer.

His mother decided to leave after he got back in the bed. About forty-five minutes later, I noticed that he was once again struggling to breathe. I gave him the morphine that the doctor had ordered for him, but he still wasn't getting any better. I called hospice, and the nurse was at my house within ten minutes. I was so glad.

The hospice nurse took over. She said that I had done all that I could do and that she needed to start administering the medicines to him now. I was terribly frightened. My husband was able to talk to me, but he was fighting to breathe.

I told him that I was going to fix him some dinner. I started to prepare a pot of lentil soup because he couldn't eat anything heavy. The hospice nurse sat with him while I prepared dinner. He said that he wanted some ice cream. I asked the nurse if he could have some, and she said yes. She said that I could give him whatever he thought he could eat. We only had a package of Nutty Buddies in the refrigerator, so I gave him the ice cream from one of the cones. He smiled as I fed him the ice cream, telling me how good it was.

After a while, he went to sleep. He was drifting between sleep and wakefulness. I just watched him. He woke up and asked me to get in the bed with him. I asked him if he was getting frisky, and he said yes and laughed. I wanted to lie beside him, but I knew he was too sick at this point. I told him that I would join him later once he felt better. He went back to sleep.

I noticed that he had stopped talking. His eyes were opened. He wanted to talk, but he couldn't. He signaled with his hands to give him something to write with because he had something to say. I did. He wrote the word "water" on a piece of paper. I got the water and give him a straw to drink the water. After that, he didn't do anything else.

As the evening progressed, I felt as though I could barely hold on. I was so scared and tired. The hospice nurse told me to lie down for a while, promising to call me if anything changed, good or bad. She said that I needed to get some rest. So I lay down on the sofa in the family room not far from his bed. I couldn't sleep. I just prayed. He was suffering now. He couldn't breathe on his own at all. I just wanted him to feel better. All I could think of was how he had talked about us going to Paris the next year for our vacation. He told me that he wasn't going to die and that he was going to beat the cancer. He was so afraid, but he was determined to live. He said that he would not leave me alone. We had finally gotten our marriage together, and we were going to get old together; that's what he had said to me in Florida. We had just had that conversation earlier this morning again, and now he was fighting for his life.

He rested all of the evening and into the next morning, which was Sunday, November 15. I didn't sleep at all. I just watched him all night.

I was hoping that he would be better the next day, since he had slept all of the night. He wasn't talking at all now. I just wanted to hear his voice. I talked to him, but he couldn't respond. The hospice nurse said that he could hear me but he was just too weak to respond. I stood by his bed. The hospice nurse told me that I needed to get some rest. She told me to lie down for a while and that she would call me if anything changed.

Later on, the hospice nurse called me and told me to come into the room. I jumped up and went to his bed where she stood over him. Then she said the most chilling words to me. "It's time. You need to pull all of his family together because he doesn't have long to live now." She told me to feel his stomach. I did, and it was as hard as a brick. She repeated that he didn't have much longer to live. I was numb. I called his family and my family.

The house was now filled with people, but I stayed in the room with my husband. I closed the door for privacy and watch him struggle to breathe. It was awful. He was suffering so much now. My tears just poured from me like a river. I only thought about how much I loved him and wanted him to get better. I felt like he was really slipping away from me now, and I couldn't stop it from happening. I didn't want him to leave me alone. I just cried and cried. I could barely stand up now. My husband was going to leave me, and I wanted to go with him at that point. I knew my son still needed me, but I was just in a zone that was unexplainable.

I could hear the family talking in the next room. I don't even know if they understood the seriousness of the situation yet. I remembered thinking, *How can they be talking about anything other than what is happening in the room with my husband?* He was fighting to live, and that was all that mattered now. Absolutely nothing else should matter.

I watched as my husband continued to fight to breathe. The hospice nurse was on the left side of him bed, and I was on his right side. She walked over to me and whispered in my ear. She told me that I needed to tell him that he needed to leave now. She explained to me that he would go on the rest of the evening fighting to breathe and that he was suffering too much now. She told me to tell him that he needed to go home now. Even as I put this on paper now, it breaks my heart; I remember every moment as though it was just yesterday, and it's almost been three years now. But I couldn't tell him to leave. I understood that he was suffering, but I just didn't want him to go. I was still holding onto hope that something miraculous was going to happen.

I continued to watch him. His head was positioned to the left, as the nurse had walked back to that side of the bed. She told me to talk to him because he could hear me—that the hearing was the last thing to go. I could barely open my mouth. I was thinking that I wasn't going to tell him to go home. I found some words somehow.

I remember telling him that I loved him so much. I asked him to open his eyes if he could hear me. He just continued to fight to breathe. I then said to him, "Baby, I want you to be at peace now." That's exactly what I told him. I kept repeating that to him. I told him that I was right by his side and that he was to be at peace and stop fighting.

I said to him, "If you can hear me, baby, please open your eyes. I love you so much. I am right here with you." I repeated this several times. The hospice nurse told me again, "He can hear you." She told me to keep talking to him.

After five minutes of telling him how much I loved him and to open his eyes if he could hear me, I noticed that he struggled to move his head to the right side, where I stood rubbing his arm. As he struggled for breath, his head moved slowly toward my voice. His eyes opened slowly, and as he looked at me, one tear rolled down his face. His eyes opened wide to see me, and he took his last breath.

"He is gone," the nurse said.

I just screamed at the top of my lungs. I couldn't stop screaming. I don't know how to explain that moment; it was just pure grief. At that moment, I couldn't understand why he had to die. He wasn't supposed to die. Then I thought, *He's not really dead. This is a dream.* My mind was racing, as though I had entered another dimension in time. This wasn't really happening. I remember thinking that the nightmare was going to be over any minute and he was going to get up out of that bed.

I asked the nurse if I could get into bed with him because I remembered telling him yesterday that I would get in the bed with him. I wrapped my body over his and just held him tightly. I didn't want to let him go. I prayed that he would be received into heaven. I just prayed. The hospice nurse told me I needed to let him go. I didn't want to. I remembered her pulling me off of him.

I remember someone—I can't even recall who—coming into the room and taking me out of the room. I went outside while the nurse prepared him for whatever needed to be done. I remember being outside and screaming and crying like a mad woman. I felt that the world should be suffering because of his death. I felt as though the entire neighborhood should feel my grief. Yet, no one in the neighborhood even knew us. I didn't care. They still should be hurting; at least, that's how I felt. My husband had died, and no one should be happy right now. I had lost my husband.

I remember my sister trying to calm me down outside. Then I turned around and saw them bring him out in the bag. That was it for me. I knew he was claustrophobic and that he wouldn't want to be in the bag. Despite the fact that he was dead, I didn't want him in that bag. I guess I was acting crazy at this point, but I didn't care. At this point, I felt lost—I mean totally lost. I was numb all over.

I remember nothing of the rest of that day—November 15, 2009.

CHAPTER **11**

Living by Faith

The next day seemed overwhelming, as it was time to prepare for the funeral. I decided to just let his family take the lead. I had nothing in me anyway. As the family gathered at my home to make all of the arrangements, I felt as though nothing mattered anymore. I went through the motions of talking about the funeral with his family. I felt unfocused and didn't care about much at that point, yet I knew that I had to take some responsibility for his funeral.

After all the arrangements had been made by his family, I tried not to break down. Every day was a battle to get through. I couldn't even pray at that point. I just felt numb. I don't remember much of what I did each day before the funeral. Life just seemed pointless then.

I do remember preparing a letter to him to be read for his eulogy. I wasn't able to say much that day, but one of my friends read the letter for me. It didn't take me long to write it. In fact, I did it a couple of hours before his funeral. I wanted to say my good-byes in my own way. Here's what I wrote:

My dear husband,

On January 4, 2008, our world changed when you were diagnosed with terminal lung cancer. We cried together that day. It was a horrible blow. We had just moved into our beautiful new home.

But we decided to trust God and believe the best in spite of the attack. Our love grew closer and closer and closer. We became inseparable. When you suffered, I suffered. Yet your strength was amazing to so many people.

You were determined to live, and you tried so hard to keep your dreams alive. We talked about our plans for the future, such as to visit Paris and go to Disney World. We made it to Disney World, and it was magical for you. And I enjoyed watching the glow in your eyes because this was your dream.

In the past couple of months, you have suffered so much, but you kept on believing that you would live. And yet you tried to prepare me to exist without you, just in case you didn't.

You told me so many times that you wouldn't leave me. And on your last day, you fought hard to live in spite of your suffering.

As I held onto you on that day, I realized that you couldn't leave me. You will always be with me. And even as I watched you take your last breath, I knew in my heart that you would somehow still be with me. That's why I didn't say good-bye then to you. I told you to be at peace.

I still won't say good-bye, but rather, until later …

These were the words that came to my heart for his eulogy.

I remembered kissing him before the funeral director closed his casket and feeling totally numb. I floated the entire day. I felt lifeless. I knew I had to make it through the funeral, but it wasn't easy.

My son came home for the funeral and for the Thanksgiving holiday, which was the following week. I was so glad to have him home with me. He helped me a lot. I knew that I had to be strong because of him. He was my reason I wanted to keep on living. Nothing else mattered anymore.

After taking a week off of work to prepare for my husband's funeral, I had to go back to work. I had to go back because I wasn't getting paid to take off for his funeral. I only had my income, and the bills would continue. I simply couldn't afford to take two weeks off, even though I needed to be at home for a while.

I really didn't want to be at work. I was hurting so much inside, but I had to be strong. I just stayed focused. When I felt as though I needed to cry, I just went to the restroom and cried. I spent a lot of time in the restroom. I didn't want my coworkers to see me breakdown. There were times throughout the day that I had a hard time holding back the tears. But everyone understood. My boss was very understanding, and she was very comforting to me during that time. Thank God I had a good boss.

I really did need time at home to grieve, but there just wasn't time. I couldn't afford to stay at home and grieve. I had so many responsibilities on me now, especially the extremely huge mortgage payment. I didn't want to lose my home now. My husband wanted us to keep our home, and he tried so hard, even until his death. My fight for our home was now about him. I had to continue to fight foreclosure. It was important to me because my husband had spent his last days here on this earth trying to hold onto our new home.

My life now seemed to take on a whole new meaning. I felt drawn to get closer to my God. One night, about a week after his death, I turned on the television and tuned into an inspirational program. As part of the program, a choir was singing praise and worship music, and I recognized many of the songs from my church. I sat up in the bed and begin to sing along. It really lifted my spirit. I got out of my bed and stood on the floor and worshipped. This gave me so much comfort. I realized that this was my hope for my future. I had to live by faith. It was just me now. I was alone. My son had gone back to school, and I was all alone in a big house. It was my God and me. I made a decision that I would walk by faith. That's all I knew. My husband's death was the end and beginning of a new life.

CHAPTER 12

My Purpose

It was a new year now. I had made it through the Thanksgiving and Christmas holidays. It was really hard to believe that my husband was gone. A part of me was waiting for him to come home. It sort of felt as though he had been away for his summer camp for the Army National Guard.

I realized that I only existed. I went to work, came home, and prepared for the next day. Over the weekend, I stayed inside, and on Sunday, I went to church. I followed the same regiment day after day. Some weekends, I didn't talk to anyone. I didn't answer my phone if it rang because I didn't want to talk to anyone at all. I figured, if I had to go to work and act as if nothing was wrong with me, then I should be able to be at home and not pretend as if everything was okay. I was tired and overwhelmed with creditors threatening me.

I refused to go to the mailbox on Fridays because I didn't want my weekends to be consumed with worrying about the bills. I felt so embarrassed about my appearance. The circles under my eyes looked bad. I wanted to pull myself together. But finding the motivation was hard. I couldn't lose any weight because I ate so late every night after work and went straight to bed. I had no energy to exercise.

I knew for a fact that, if I didn't stay strong and hold onto my faith in God, I would not be able to handle the pressure and all the obstacles I was facing. Yet, I didn't know my place anymore. Where did I belong? What was my purpose? I was no longer a wife. No one needed me. My son had gone back to campus, and I was all alone. I just felt so lost.

As I reflected back to the fifth blade that I could not see, I somehow began to understand why it was so important to hold onto my faith. I couldn't see straight at that point in my life. My life had dark areas, and I had to deal with them.

Somehow, I couldn't help thinking that the unseen blade represented what I couldn't see coming. Events would be coming, and I was going to have to make a lot of adjustments in my life. I tried so hard to understand why things happened the way they had, and yet I couldn't make any sense out of it. Simple reminders of the little things my husband used to do would make me sad.

Every time I went to the gas station, I thought about him. I had to laugh to myself because he would always tell me that all I did was get in the car and drive it. He was right. He would take care of all of the automobiles. Now I had to smile every time I pumped gas.

Nighttime seemed to be the hardest. I had a habit of still waiting for him to come home. I would go into the empty room that he died in and just sit on the floor. For a strange reason, I was hoping that his spirit would come back and visit with me. I missed him so much. I wanted to see him again. Yet I knew to be absent from the body is to be present with the Lord. I still would look for signs to see if he had come back to see me. Realizing that we had a lot of marital problems, we had both fought to keep our marriage going. We shut out the world to build a solid relationship, and we were determined to be there for each other, no matter what. I sometimes believed that he didn't want anyone around us, because he didn't want anyone or anything to get in our way of trying to grow together. It was unfortunate because I learned so much about him after his death. Things about his past were revealed to me that I'd had no idea about. It didn't matter because I loved him anyway. Nothing was going to change how I felt.

The fact now was that I had to start all over again. I had decided that I would fight foreclosure—despite the fact that I was faced with a daily barrage of bill collectors calling me and certified letters coming in the mail, threatening to foreclose on my home. I was scared. I had only my faith to keep me strong. Financial consultants and practically everyone who knew about my situation advised me to walk away from my home. The responsibility was too much for one person. I stopped reading the mail and just did everything I knew to do to get a modification for a new loan.

Whenever I wanted to know what was going on with the modification, I just called the bank. Reading the mail from the bank always seemed to be so intimidating. Talking with someone on the phone was easier for me to handle than actually reading the mail.

Somehow, I got through it. I got the modification for my loan, but it was for every dime of my paycheck. I would have nothing to live on after paying the mortgage. What a life. The struggles just seemed to keep coming after he died. I wanted to give up so many times, but I had the fifth blade on my mind all the time. I believed that hope was there—it was coming; but when? This was the problem that I had to deal with every day. When was happiness coming?

CHAPTER 13

The Pearl

The year 2010 went by so quickly. I worked very hard and didn't miss a day of work. I struggled every week to keep the bills paid. My credit score had taken a huge nosedive, and that made me very unhappy. I had to make myself come to terms with that because I was doing the best I knew how with what money I had. I still had the same regimen. Nothing changed. I worked every day and went to church on Sunday. That was pretty much my life.

Before I knew it, another year was here, and it was time for my son to graduate from college. I was so happy about him completing his four years on time and getting his degree. It was hard for him to see his mother struggle. He wanted to see me get out of the house some and do some things. I didn't know how anymore. Happiness didn't seem important anymore now. I just went through life working to pay bills. At least that seemed to be the main focus. I worked to make sure everybody was paid. And once the company I was working for allowed its contractors to work unlimited overtime, I took advantage of that opportunity. The overtime allowed me to pay on all of my bills. Nothing was left but I wanted to clean my credit up. I believed then and still believe that I'd made the bills and it was my responsibility to pay them off.

After my son's graduation, he came back home. We hadn't spent much time together since my husband's death. With him home, I felt so much better. I wasn't alone anymore. I had someone to talk to now. And moreover, my son and I were able to talk about something we'd not yet discussed—how all this had affected him. I had talked to him during his vacations at home about the struggles that I was faced with every month, and he'd heard me complain about the mortgage company every time he called. But it wasn't until then that I learned the depth of his concern for me. He had been profoundly worried, and I hadn't realized that. I guess I'd just thought that, as he was away, he was removed from the everyday drama of my life; I'd hoped that, not exposed to the days and night that I cried out to the Lord for help, he would just stay focused on his schoolwork and not think about me. Now I discovered that he had been worrying about me all the time. Having him there at that time was a blessing. We needed each other.

Things seemed to be changing as a new year approached. The end of 2011 was a little bit better since my son was home with me. I was Mom. I had someone to cook for, and I had someone to talk to everyday. I still didn't go anywhere. He kept encouraging me to get out of the house and to try to meet new people. I had no desire to go anywhere. I was happy with being at home. But I knew that he would be leaving one day to start his own life. So I was going to have to start living again on my own. Being a single woman seemed frightening to me. Even after so much time had passed since my husband died, I was still holding onto my love for him. I still dreamed about him coming back. I was still missing him—so much that looking at his pictures hurt. To me, as long as I had the pictures of him throughout the house, it meant that I didn't have to let go. I didn't want to let go.

Going to work every day kept me focused. Occasionally, I would think back to that job with the federal government that I had wanted and how the agency had possibly chosen not to hire me because of my baggage; I knew I would have put my heart into that job. In fact, I went to work every day and had only missed the one week to bury my husband. I made it through all of the bad weather; worked on Saturdays to make up time for holidays; and went to work sick, even after falling down the steps and injuring my leg. I was dedicated and would have done the same with that agency. Paying the mortgage and the other bills were my main priorities, and I felt blessed to have a job, even if it was a long-term temporary assignment.

My son and I talked about me trying to start dating. I did want 2012 to start off right, but I didn't know if that meant trying to get out a little. I wanted to start looking for a new job with benefits. That's the change I wanted.

Things were about to change again in 2012. My son decided to go back to campus to work on his master's degree. I was going to be alone again. I was okay with that because we had talked about him pursuing his dream. I wasn't going to get in the way of his education. I had to try to make it on my own again. I did feel stronger now. My faith was my pearl. But I was still lonesome and still holding onto my love for my husband. I prepared myself to be alone, and I didn't feel sad about that either. I decided that I would try to work on writing my book that I had started some years ago. That meant a lot to me.

It was time for my son to prepare to go back to campus. We went to the grocery store to pick up a few things for him to take back to school. As soon as I got into the store, I ran into an old friend from high school. I shared my grief about losing my husband. We talked a little bit, and I explained that I had to take my son back to school in a few days. We talked about going to the school track to walk because we had run into each other on the track some years ago before my husband had died.

I wasn't quite sure if I wanted to meet this friend at the track; I just wasn't comfortable with anyone. I had grown to lack trust in people after being alone for so long. I couldn't seem to come up with a good excuse not to meet at the track, though, so I said that I would be there.

As soon as I got home, I changed my mind and was very sorry that I had set up a time to meet at the track. I felt happier now, yet I was a little confused about my purpose. I decided to talk to God about my decision. I went to the family room and looked up at the five blades on the ceiling fan and thought to myself, *Now what is it that I am not seeing or need to see?*

My old friend and I did make it to the track, and we walked 10 miles. We talked about everything, including my strong desire to finish my book. But what was the most surprising thing to learn was that he had the same pearl.